Lovey Bunny

Kristine A. Lombardi

Abrams Books for Young Readers
New York

The art in this book was created in pencil
and gouache and then digitally colored.

Library of Congress Cataloging-in-Publication Data

Lombardi, Kristine A.
Lovey bunny / by Kristine A. Lombardi.
pages cm
Summary: A young rabbit who loves playing dress-up ruins the special dress her Mama just finished making, then uses her craft supplies to fix it and become her mother's "lovey bunny" again.
ISBN 978-1-4197-1485-6
[1. Mother and child—Fiction. 2. Clothing and dress—Fiction.]
I. Title.
PZ7.L83316Lov 2015
[E]—dc23
2014017027

Book design by Chad W. Beckerman

Published in 2015 by Abrams Books for Young Readers, an imprint of ABRAMS.

Printed and bound in China
10 9 8 7 6 5 4 3 2

115 West 18th Street
New York, NY 10011
www.abramsbooks.com

To my mom & dad
and the childhood
you gave me

THIS
END UP

I'm such a lovey bunny!
Mama tells me so.

I love just about EVERYTHING!

I love
my family.
43

I love to sit
and read.
I love the
SUN!

I love
ART!
CRAYON

flour
I love helping Mama.
I love watching Mama make stuff.

BERGDORF
But I really love
to play dress up!

and pretend
I'm grown up.
Body Souffle

One day, there was something special hanging on Mama's closet door.

I simply had to try it on!

I'm such a
glamorous bunny!

I looked pretty, just like Mama—

too pretty to stay in the house.

So I went outside and waved to all my admirers.

I got so caught up in the moment

that I didn't even notice...

I had ruined Mama's dress!

I tried to sneak back inside, but Mama was waiting.

My dress! It took months to make. Now what will I wear to the party tonight?

Am I still Mama's lovey bunny?

But then I have an idea.

Will Mama even notice the difference?

I couldn't wait to show her!

How beautiful! I LOVE it! Thank you, my lovey bunny!

Mama stays home tonight to cook a special dinner for everyone.

Mama loves her dress and...

I'll always be her lovey bunny.